The Hidden Dagger

by Margo Sorenson

To Jim, Jane, and Jill who always believed this would happen.
To Dr. Bryce Lyon who made history come alive.

M. S.

Cover Illustration: Donna Rae Nelson
Inside Illustration: Michael A. Aspengren

10 PP 09 08 07 06 05

Contents

Background Summary

England in Walter's time, almost 400 years ago, was very different from today. Queen Elizabeth I ruled England with an iron hand. Lords had a lot of power in England too. They could tell most everyone what to do. Some of the lords looked down on other people. The countryside was also different. Castles dotted the land. Villages were small. There weren't many cities. Most people were farmers. They farmed on land that belonged to the lords. People had to be rich to own their own land. Raising sheep and weaving cloth were important too. Cloth made a lot of money for England. England was a proud and powerful nation in 1600.

1

The Threat

Walter tensed his muscles. What was going on in the other room? The angry voices echoed in the castle.

"I told you before! *No!*"

"You greedy dog!"

Two men were arguing in the great hall. Walter listened and frowned. He knew what happened when grown men got angry. Daggers were poised. Glittering swords were drawn. Often, blood was spilled.

Walter liked stories about sword fighting and battles.

He wanted to be a knight when he grew older. He couldn't wait to fight in real battles. He also liked to make up his own stories about battles. He frowned. Some people thought he made up too many stories.

But right now, this was just a little too close for him. Walter clutched the cloth he was holding. He was delivering it to the castle for his father.

He hoped the men didn't know he was waiting in the small room next door. He knew he shouldn't be hearing this. He could be in danger just by being there. Angry men didn't like witnesses.

He could just imagine one of the men raising a dagger. The blade would flash in the firelight. Then it would slash downward. Blood would be spilled. He shuddered.

The voices were getting louder. He was sure someone was going to get hurt. If only he could just sneak away. But his father had told him to deliver the cloth. The seamstress needed it to sew more clothes for Lord Fanshaw and his family.

"I will *not!*" A man's voice rang out. It sounded like Lord Fanshaw's voice, and he sounded furious! Walter wondered who could make Lord Fanshaw so angry.

Thud! Walter heard a fist pound on heavy wood. Walter shrank back against the stone castle wall, still clutching the cloth. He was glad he wasn't in the same room with the two men. He wanted them to stop. What if something awful happened? What if they fought with daggers or swords?

"You must!" the other voice raged. "As my brother, you must do it!"

He said "brother." The other man must be Thomas, Lord Fanshaw's brother. Walter knew about him. Everyone in the small village talked about Thomas. He was no good—a "blackguard" they called him.

"It isn't fair! It's never been fair! You got everything from father—the land, the money—everything! Just because you are the oldest," Thomas went on. His voice sounded hoarse.

"You chose to go into the army," Lord Fanshaw argued. "You could have had a good life in the army. Instead, you're nothing but a drunkard!"

"I am *not*," Thomas roared. "I can't live on the allowance you give me. It's not enough to feed a mouse!"

"If you wouldn't drink it up every month, it would be enough!" Lord Fanshaw snapped.

"You'll be sorry for that," Thomas threatened.

What does he mean by that? Walter wondered. Thomas sounded deadly serious. He wasn't—he wasn't thinking about doing something to his brother, was he?

"That's it. You're not getting another cent from me!" Lord Fanshaw said. Walter heard a book close with a thump. "You are on your own, my brother."

"You'll regret this," Thomas repeated. "I could *kill* you!"

Walter listened in horror. Kill? Thomas had said *kill!* He could picture the two men. Thomas would draw his dagger. He would stab his brother. Walter felt helpless and frightened. He couldn't believe this. It had to stop!

Lord Fanshaw laughed coldly. It sent shivers down Walter's spine. "You?" he sneered. "You're a weakling!"

"By the Queen's blood, I'll make sure you regret this," Thomas threatened. The sound of a fist hitting wood echoed again on the stone castle walls. Next, Walter heard the jangling and clanking of a dagger being buckled. Or was it being unbuckled?

Walter froze. Thomas wasn't going to draw his dagger, was he? Thomas wasn't going to kill Lord Fanshaw right now, was he? Walter's blood ran cold. What could he do? He was too young to stop a murder! He could just imagine a scream from Lord Fanshaw and then the dull thud of a body falling to the floor.

Suddenly, Thomas appeared at the door of the room where Walter stood. He stared hard at Walter for a moment. There was hate in his eyes. He was breathing hard. "What's this? An eavesdropper?"

Walter couldn't move and couldn't speak. His feet felt nailed to the floor. His tongue stuck to the roof of his mouth in fear.

Then Thomas sneered. "Huh! Just a young pup from the village." He looked at the cloth Walter was carrying. "Delivering cloth, eh? You'll be lucky to get paid *here*." Then he brushed Walter aside. His cloak rippled after him.

Walter's fear was replaced by anger. He hated it when rich people treated him like dirt. He was just as good as anybody. He held his head high. He didn't need a castle or a fancy title like "Lord this" or "Duke that." Being plain Walter Poresby was good enough for him.

His father, Robert Poresby, made a good living as a clothier. He sold cloth to lords and ladies and gentlemen. Sometimes he even sent cloth to London to sell. Walter knew the Poresbys weren't rich, but they weren't poor either.

"Who are you?" A girl's voice interrupted his thoughts. Walter looked up. He felt his face flush. It was Lord Fanshaw's daughter, Lady Anne. She was close to his younger sister's age—about 13.

But she sure didn't dress or look like Walter's sister. In fact, she looked very different from the other girls in the village. All of Walter's friends talked about how beautiful she was. Walter sighed. Someone like Lady Anne would never look twice at a Walter Poresby.

"Are you deaf?" Lady Anne asked rudely. "I said, who are you?"

Walter tightened his lips. He bit back a smart answer. He took a deep breath. He had to calm down. His heart was still pumping from the scene between Thomas and Lord Fanshaw.

"Walter Poresby," he said.

"Really?" Lady Anne suddenly looked interested. "Don't you go to grammar school with my brother?"

"Yes, Milady," Walter answered. He tried to force a smile. Lady Anne's brother was Master Edward. Walter hated Edward. He acted like he was king instead of a lord's son. Walter almost snorted.

"My brother says you're really smart," Lady Anne said. "Are you?"

Walter shrugged. How could he answer a question like that? "I don't know," he said.

"He said you're always making up splendid stories," she said. Her eyes sparkled. "Can you tell me one?" she begged.

"Lady Anne!" Lord Fanshaw appeared in the room. His face darkened. "Don't you have better things to do?"

Anne looked down at her satin shoes. "Yes, Father," she mumbled. She curtsied to her father. Then she quickly left. Did she give me one more glance? Walter asked himself.

"Young Poresby, right?" Lord Fanshaw barked. "Here to deliver cloth again?"

Walter nodded. His heart raced again.

"The seamstress should be here to meet you." Lord Fanshaw frowned. "Where is she?"

Walter clutched the cloth nervously.

Lord Fanshaw's eyes narrowed. "How long have you been here?" he asked.

Walter's stomach jumped into his throat. "Uh, not long, Milord," he stammered. Could Lord Fanshaw hear his heart pounding?

Lord Fanshaw looked at Walter carefully. "You didn't hear anything, did you?" he asked.

Walter's heart thudded. "Hear what, sire?" he asked.

Lord Fanshaw suddenly looked bored. "Oh, nothing," he said. He reached near the wall and pulled on a cord. A bell rang. A servant appeared.

"Fetch the seamstress. Tell her the cloth is here." Then Lord Fanshaw turned on his heel and left.

Walter felt the sweat break out on his forehead. He remembered the argument. It had sounded really dangerous. What would Lord Fanshaw and Thomas do if they knew he had heard them?

Walter frowned. Should he tell someone about Thomas' threat? His father? He worried that his father might not believe him. Since Walter liked to make up stories, people sometimes doubted his word. He could already hear his father. "Is this another one of your stories, my boy?"

Even though his father might not believe him, Walter knew he should try to tell him anyway. After all, this was *murder* Thomas was talking about! And Walter was the only one who knew.

What if Thomas actually *did* kill Lord Fanshaw? Would Walter be the cause of the murder if he didn't tell anyone? Would that make it his fault? Walter shivered a little. He had to make sure it didn't happen. Someone had to believe his story about Thomas' threat!

There was something else too. Would Thomas remember that Walter heard him threaten his brother? He had stared hard at Walter, hadn't he? Did he think Walter was a witness? If Thomas really did kill his brother, wouldn't he want to kill Walter too?

Walter felt helpless and scared. What could he do?

2

Can Will Help?

Walter slammed the door to his house. He was out of breath.

"Father!" he yelled. "Father?!"

"Walter, what is it?" His mother hurried around the corner. "You sound as if someone is hurt."

"Not yet, anyway," Walter said. He dropped the bag of coins the seamstress had given him for the cloth. "I need to talk to Father."

"He'll be home soon. He's at a weaver's cottage checking on cloth today." His mother looked at the bag of coins. "How nice that Lord Fanshaw doesn't insist on credit," she said. "So many lords and ladies won't pay us right away." She sighed. "Even the village people pay us with coin or crops. Like that nice Will Barnes," she went on. "He bought cloth last week for a new vest. He paid us in corn."

15

Will Barnes! Walter thought excitedly. That was his answer! He could talk to Will about Lord Fanshaw and Thomas. Will would listen to his story, and he would know what to do.

Although Will was much older—almost 20—Walter thought of him as his friend. Once, Walter had helped Will find his family's lost cows. Will was grateful. "You can count on me if you need help, little friend," Will had said.

And Will always seemed to have a plan for things. Maybe Will could help stop the murder. He would know what to do. He should go right now to Will's small cottage. It stood at the edge of the village. Walter was bursting with his story about the argument at the castle.

"Aha! I'm home, Mary!"

Walter heard his father's voice. His heart sank. Now he would have to wait until tomorrow to see Will. But he should probably tell his father anyway. Walter sighed. He already knew what his father would say.

Robert Poresby stamped the mud from his feet on the mat. He gave his wife a squeeze. He ruffled Walter's hair.

"Did you deliver the goods to the castle?" he asked Walter.

"Yes, Father," Walter answered. He reached for the coins on the table. "Here is the payment."

"Good, good," Robert said, smiling. "Good lad. We'll make a clothier out of you yet."

No! Walter wanted to shout. He didn't *want* to be a

clothier. It was so boring. Clothiers made sure sheep were shorn. Then they had the wool spun into yarn. Next, they had the yarn woven into cloth. Finally, they sold the cloth to people for making clothes. There was nothing more boring—unless it was reading Latin poets. Being a clothier was definitely not for him.

Walter had other plans for his life. He would wear armor for Queen Elizabeth! He wanted to fight in strange countries! He saw himself flashing swords with the enemy.

Walter looked down at the wooden-planked floor. Walter's plans for his future were no secret. Everyone in his village of Halstead knew. He made up stories all the time about knights in battle.

Sometimes Walter's stories got him into trouble. Walter often wrote about knights and battles in his copybook instead of copying the dull Latin poets. If Master Smyth caught Walter, he would cane him. Still, Walter continued making up stories and dreaming about fighting battles.

"Harrumph, my lad," Robert Poresby said. "You look as if you have something on your mind."

Walter took a deep breath. He had to tell his father what had happened at the castle. It was too scary to keep quiet about it. He had to try to stop the murder.

"Father, I overheard an argument at the castle," Walter began.

Robert frowned.

"It was Lord Fanshaw and his brother Thomas," Walter went on.

"Ah—that rascal Thomas!" his mother exclaimed.

"They were arguing about money," Walter continued.

"Now, Walter," his father interrupted. "We have brought you up to stay out of other people's business."

"But Father—" Walter began.

"No!" his father commanded. "I have heard enough. Stay out of it. Especially stay away from what happens in the castle. Their ways are different from our ways."

"But—" Walter begged.

"No!" his father roared. Walter's stomach tied into a knot. When his father was like this, Walter knew he had to obey. Once he had talked back to his father. His father had locked him in the shed for a day.

Walter hung his head. "Yes, sir. Sorry, sir."

Father doesn't understand, he thought. This murder might happen if I don't do something.

Then he remembered Will. He'd have to find him tomorrow. Walter knew his friend would be at the Four Boars Tavern in the afternoon. Tomorrow was Wednesday, and Will always went to the tavern after market day. He met other farmers there. They would talk about their crops.

Sometimes Will would talk politics with the other farmers. Will was not shy. He said exactly what was on his mind. Sometimes he said things that made others angry.

If there was a fight at the Four Boars, Will would often be in it. "Hot-blooded," people called him. But Will always had a plan for getting out of trouble.

Walter would go there right after school. He hoped it wouldn't be too late.

****

The next afternoon finally came. Walter sat impatiently at his school desk. Master Smyth was finishing with the younger boys. Walter sighed. He tapped his foot.

Walter heard a hiss behind him. "What's your hurry?" It was Master Edward, Lord Fanshaw's son.

Walter shook his head in disgust. Master Edward was a pain, and everyone knew it. Too bad his latest private tutor at the castle had quit. Walter hid a smile. Sooner or later, all of Edward's tutors quit.

In between tutors, Lord Fanshaw sent Edward to the local grammar school. That was where all the Halstead village boys went. The village girls didn't go to school. They stayed home and learned to sew or paint unless they were rich enough for a tutor—like Lady Anne.

Edward didn't fit in with the Halstead boys. Nor did he act as if he wanted to. Walter almost snorted. Edward always walked into the schoolroom with his head held high. He brushed off his seat before he sat down. Snickers from the village boys would fill the air. But Edward never seemed to notice.

"None of your business," Walter hissed back. I'm trying to save your father, idiot! he wanted to spit back.

"Poresby!" barked Master Smyth.

Uh-oh, Walter thought. He sat straight up in his chair. "Yes, sir," he said.

"Telling more of your fanciful stories? Not paying attention to your lessons?" demanded Master Smyth. He walked over and tapped his pointer sharply on Walter's desk.

"Ah—no, sir. I mean yes, sir," Walter stammered. He heard muffled laughter around him.

"Since you have time to whisper to your friends," Walter made a face at the word *friends,* "I'll give you another lesson to do." Master Smyth smiled evilly at Walter. "I want three more quotes in your Little Book for tomorrow."

Walter almost groaned aloud. All the schoolboys had to collect quotes from their reading. They had to copy them into their Little Books. The boys were to use the quotes when they wrote compositions. The quotes were sayings from the ancient Romans or Greeks. Walter especially liked the quotes about battles and fighting. He didn't mind finding those quotes to copy. But now he had to do three more than everyone else.

"Too bad, Poresby," Edward snickered behind him. Walter's blood pumped through his head. He would really like to cuff Edward a good one. He'd like to see the blood drip from Edward's nose onto his fancy clothes.

Walter stared out the window. He could just see himself jousting with Edward. He'd race his horse right toward Edward. His lance would be steady. He would be grinning under his helmet. Ka-wham! He would unseat Edward from his horse at the first pass.

Walter hid a smile. Edward was such a sissy. How did he get to be that way? His father, Lord Fanshaw, had a reputation for being tough.

Lord Fanshaw—Walter bolted up straight. He had almost forgotten what he had to do this afternoon! He had to find Will at the Four Boars. He had to tell him about Thomas and the argument. He would ask Will what to do. Should he tell Constable Hawkins, the village policeman? Should he hide from Thomas? Will would have good advice.

3

Will's Answer

Walter opened the door of the Four Boars Tavern. Hot, steamy air swirled around him. Laughter and loud men's voices filled the air.

"So your crop will be better this year, eh?" someone asked.

"Only if High-and-Mighty Lord Fanshaw lets us keep our land," a voice growled. Walter recognized Will's voice.

Walter walked around the corner. He saw Will at the center of one of the large tables in the tavern. Men crowded around the table. They drank from large mugs.

"You think this enclosure will really happen?" one of the men asked Will.

Enclosure. Walter knew what that was. It meant that Lord Fanshaw would fence off a lot of the village land for himself. As it stood, everyone in the village could farm little strips of land. But now, Lord Fanshaw wanted the land for himself. And he could do what he wanted because he was the lord. Walter frowned.

Will was still grumbling. "Lord Moneybags knows he'll make a lot more money. He'll put his sheep on our land instead of letting us farm it."

Will continued in a loud, angry voice. "He wants to fence it off for himself. Then his sheep will graze on our land—*our* land." Will's face darkened. "Wool is getting a fancy price these days. He'll make more money for himself. We won't make as much money from our crops."

"It's not fair!" said another man. "It would be the worst thing to ever happen in our village!"

"Aye," said another man. "We'll soon starve."

"I'll make sure we won't starve," Will said angrily. "I'll take care of Lord Fanshaw before that happens."

The men around the table grew silent. They looked at each other.

Finally, one of the men spoke up. "Now, Will, ye won't do anything foolish?"

Will banged his fist on the table. His mug jumped. Ale sloshed onto the table. "I'll do what I have to do! The enclosure won't happen here!"

The men grunted to each other.

Walter blinked. Had Will just threatened Lord Fanshaw's life? He shook his head. No, Will would never do anything that foolish. He had just said he would "take care" of him. Whatever that meant.

"Well, here's a lad to join us!" One of the village men was grinning at Walter. The talking stopped. All eyes were on Walter.

Walter's face turned warm.

"Have a mug of ale, lad?" another man joked. "Care to join our conversation?"

"Aye, maybe he has an idea what to do with Lord Fanshaw!" a third man said, grinning. "Tell your father not to buy Lord Fanshaw's wool!"

Walter bit his lip. He couldn't tell his father that. His father would buy the best wool wherever he could. Walter felt torn. He knew the men were right. But he knew his father needed wool too.

"Don't tease the lad," Will said. He smiled at Walter. " 'Tis not his fault. Besides, I'll take care of the problem."

"Aye," one of the men agreed. "If ever a man can do it, it's you, Will."

A chorus of "Aye" and "That's right" filled the air. Then the men began talking about crops again.

Will ignored the others. He looked at Walter. "So

what can I do for you?" Will asked, smiling.

Walter looked around at the men talking to each other. "Can we talk somewhere else? I don't want to say it here," he said nervously.

Will's smile faded. "Trouble, lad?" he asked. "With that dolt Master Edward, I suppose."

"Let's go outside," Walter said. Will pushed his stool away from the table. Together, Will and Walter walked out into the brisk air.

"Well, little friend, what is it?" Will asked.

Walter looked around carefully. No one was in sight on the narrow road. He took a deep breath.

"I—I was at the castle yesterday," he began.

Will frowned.

"I was delivering cloth for my father," Walter went on. "I was waiting in a little room off the great hall. I heard angry voices. Two men were arguing. One was Lord Fanshaw. The other was his brother Thomas."

"Thomas! That lying, lily-livered—" Will began. He saw Walter's face and stopped. "Sorry, lad. Go ahead."

"Anyway, Thomas wanted more money for his allowance. Lord Fanshaw told him no. Then—" Walter stopped. He took another breath. "Then, Thomas said that he would kill him! I thought he was going to do it right then!"

Will looked thoughtful. "And then what?" he asked.

Walter swallowed hard. "Then Thomas rushed out. And he saw me waiting in the next room! I think he knows I heard everything."

Will frowned. "I think I see your problem," he said.

"If I don't say anything to anyone, Thomas might kill Lord Fanshaw. And it would be my fault because I could stop the murder." Walter looked worried. "But if I *do* say something, Thomas would know it was me. And if Thomas *does* kill Lord Fanshaw, I'm almost a witness. Thomas might come after me. What do I do?" Walter asked desperately.

Will folded his arms. Then he walked a little way down the road. Walter watched as Will bent his head in thought. He turned around and came back.

"Here now, Walter," he began. "Lord Fanshaw is a big man. He can take care of himself. You don't need to protect him. You don't need to tell Constable Hawkins— or anyone else for that matter. Lord Fanshaw has men who can guard him if he thinks he needs it."

Will is right, Walter thought. Why hadn't he thought of that?

"If Thomas *does* kill him, he'll probably leave the country for a while. He may forget about you. He'll be more worried about saving his own skin than remembering a village lad."

"But he knows I heard him," Walter worried aloud. "He might think about killing me too."

"Yes, that's possible," Will agreed. "Thomas is such a blackguard. He probably *would* think nothing of killing a boy." Will's forehead creased in thought. "I'll tell you what. If Thomas does kill him, I'll be sure to help you. Until they catch Thomas, you may need to hide. I'll find a place for you to hide. But until then, don't worry."

"You don't think he would try to kill me *before* he killed Lord Fanshaw, do you?" Walter asked.

"No," Will said. "He is stupid, true. But I don't think he's that stupid. He wouldn't risk killing you—unless he had already killed Lord Fanshaw. Then he would have nothing to lose by killing you. He would already be a murderer anyway."

Walter shuddered a little. This was terrible.

Will leaned against the tavern wall. He grinned at Walter. "Besides, it's more important to him to kill his brother. He'll get all the lands and money if he does. If he's going to have his head chopped off for murder, he'd rather have it chopped off for that. He wouldn't want his head chopped off for just *your* murder!" Will grinned.

In spite of himself, Walter grinned back. Here he was smiling about his own possible murder! Will was like that, though. He always made things look better. Walter sighed in relief. He was still worried, but not as much.

"Thanks, Will. You're a true friend," Walter said gratefully.

"No problem, lad," Will said, grinning. "Take off, now. Your father will be wondering where you are!"

Will was right, Walter thought. He hurried down the road and turned down the lane leading to his house.

His father was unsaddling his horse. He frowned at

Walter.

"Where have ye been?" he asked. He lifted the saddle from the horse. "Ye should have been home from school before now."

"Uh, I ran into Will Barnes," Walter said quickly.

He couldn't tell his father he went to the tavern to find Will. Then his father would want to know why. And his father had told him to stay out of the Fanshaws' business. Walter felt his stomach give a little flip. He did not want his father to find out he had disobeyed him. Even though he was trying to stop a murder—and save himself.

"Will Barnes, eh?" Robert Poresby's face darkened. "I want you to stay out of trouble. And Will Barnes is trouble. Especially right now. He's been talking too much around the village. I hear he has been saying things against Lord Fanshaw." Robert's eyes narrowed. "He doesn't like the idea of Lord Fanshaw fencing off his land to raise more sheep."

Robert brushed the side of his horse. He gave it a slap on the rear. "I think it's too bad the villagers will lose some of the common land they have been using. But—" Robert frowned—"after all, it *is* the lord's land to do with as he chooses."

"Yes, sir," Walter said.

"Will has always said too much. This time, I fear he'll really be in trouble."

Will? thought Walter. His father should hear what

Thomas had threatened. He sighed. There was nothing he could do right now anyway.

"So," his father continued, "you stay away from Will Barnes. Until things settle down around the village."

Walter looked down at the muddy ground beneath his feet.

"Son? Do you hear me?" Robert repeated.

"Yes, sir," Walter said slowly. Now what was he going to do? He couldn't talk to Will if something happened. What if Thomas saw Walter around the village? What if Thomas stared at him in that terrible way again?

What if Lord Fanshaw was found dead?

4

Danger for Will

"Poresby!" barked Master Smyth the next day in school. "Read your quotes from your Little Book!"

Walter's stomach tied into a knot. He had forgotten! In all the excitement over talking to Will and worrying about Thomas, he had forgotten to do his schoolwork. He held back a shudder. Now he would be caned for sure.

Master Smyth kept a long stick or cane behind his desk. When he thought one of the boys was bad, he brought it out. Then Master Smyth swatted the boy on his backside. Sometimes it was 10 or 20 times. If someone was really bad, it could even be 50 times! Walter knew he hadn't been *that* bad!

Walter hated caning. Sometimes he thought Master Smyth became a schoolmaster just so he could cane boys. He almost seemed to smile when he brought out the cane.

"Uh, Master Smyth, sir,—" Walter stopped.

Master Smyth grinned evilly. "Yes, Poresby? You don't have your work, do you?" He bent down. He reached behind his desk. He fumbled for the cane. Then he stood up. The dreaded cane was in his hand.

"Maybe this will help you remember your lessons. I suppose you were busy making up more of your foolish stories about knights and battles instead?"

"Uh, no, sir." Walter fibbed, "My father had some work for me to do. It was for Lord Fanshaw." Walter noticed Master Smyth's eyes brighten when he heard Lord Fanshaw's name.

"He said I had to do it. That's why I couldn't do my quotes, sir," he finished. He looked hopefully at Master Smyth. With any luck, Master Smyth might believe him. He did know Robert Poresby did business with Lord Fanshaw. And Master Smyth was always trying to impress Lord Fanshaw or anyone else at the castle.

Master Smyth frowned. He lowered the cane in his hand.

"Well, I suppose business comes first in your house," he said. He sounded disappointed, Walter thought. "But," Master Smyth went on, "you'll do *six* quotes tonight. And I'll make sure they get done. You'll stay after school to do them. Then you'll have no excuses."

Walter slumped in his chair. He sighed with relief. Whew! he thought. He had saved himself from a caning.

"Too bad he put the cane away," Master Edward hissed in his ear. "I was looking forward to it!"

Walter's blood boiled. It would be so easy to turn Edward's face into a bloody pulp, he thought. Edward would be crying for mercy. He'd be whimpering into that lace handkerchief of his.

Walter glanced at Master Smyth. He was busy with some of the younger boys. Good, Walter thought.

"Shut up," Walter whispered out of the side of his mouth. "You idiot!"

"You—you peasant!" Edward sputtered.

That was it! Peasant! "Settle this after school," he threatened Edward in a low, angry voice.

"Of course not," Edward said with his nose in the air. "I don't talk to peasants outside of school."

"I am not a peasant!" Walter fumed.

"Everyone, outside," called Master Smyth. "Time for some fresh air."

Just in time, Walter thought. He shoved up against

Edward as they went out the door. Edward bumped against the doorway.

"Hey!" Edward pouted. "Leave me alone!"

"What's the matter?" Walter sneered. "Can't stand to be with the lower classes, Your Royal Highness?"

Edward's face turned red. "I'm more royal than you'll ever be!" he exclaimed. He lifted his chin. "I'll make sure my father hears about this. He won't want me treated like this."

"And then what?" Walter snapped. "He'll send his knights down to finish me off? I don't think so."

"My father knows all about the troublemakers in the village. He takes care of them. He makes sure they don't cause any more trouble. Like that stupid farmer Will Barnes," Edward sneered. "*He's* a friend of yours, isn't he? Funny how the peasant troublemakers stick together."

Walter felt the blood rush to his forehead. Stop, he told himself. He had to hear what was coming next.

"Barnes thinks he can tell my father what do with his own land." Edward tossed his head. "Hah!" he said. Then he smiled secretively. "Barnes talks too much. But soon Barnes won't be a problem anymore." He glared at Walter. "*That's* what being a lord is all about."

Will *is* in danger, then. Walter thought quickly. He had to warn Will somehow. But right now, he wanted to take care of Edward.

"Enough!" Walter commanded. He glanced up to see where Master Smyth was. Then Walter moved quickly to the left. As he did, he jabbed Edward and shoved him, hard.

Splat! Edward landed in a puddle of mud.

"You—you—" Edward stammered in fury.

Look at his fancy clothes now, Walter thought, pleased. I bet even his lace handkerchief is muddy.

"So sorry!" Walter lied. He reached out a hand to help Edward up. Edward ignored it. He struggled to get up.

"Master Edward! Master Edward!" Master Smyth came rushing over. He looked worried.

Humph, Walter snorted to himself. Master Smyth is probably worried about getting in trouble. Lord Fanshaw might be mad if his son comes home from school filthy with mud. Now Walter was really enjoying the scene. He hid a smile.

"What happened, Master Edward?" Master Smyth asked. He was wringing his hands.

"Well—" Edward began. Then he looked at Walter. Walter glared at him and made a fist with his hand. He looked down at his fist, and then he stared at Edward.

Edward met Walter's eyes. He looked nervously at Walter's fist. "Um—I just slipped," he fibbed.

Hah! Walter thought. He knows I'll beat him up if he tells. Walter almost grinned. Edward was such a sissy.

Of course, Walter wouldn't be so stupid as to beat up Edward. Lord Fanshaw would get back at Walter—or his father—if he did. But he'd do everything he could to make Edward's life miserable. That was for sure.

"You—you—dog!" Edward hissed after Master Smyth had left.

"What a silly accident," Walter lied smoothly. "I'm so clumsy."

"You're no better than the stupid farmers in this village. I don't care if your father is a clothier. You're no better than the rest of the peasant boys." Edward rubbed his elbow. He pulled out his lace handkerchief. It was wet and muddy. Still he reached down and tried to wipe some of the mud off his legs.

Walter tightened his mouth. He had to calm down. *He* knew he was better than the others. After all, he planned to be a knight someday. He would fight for the Queen and bring glory to England!

But right now, he had to find Will and warn him that Lord Fanshaw was angry with him. Then maybe Will could lie low for a while.

What evil was Lord Fanshaw planning for Will?

5

A Bloody Dagger

Walter quietly closed his front door. He didn't want his father to hear him come in. He was late, and he didn't want to explain where he'd been.

First, he had copied the extra quotes after school. Then luckily, on his way home from school, he had found Will at the Four Boars Tavern. Walter warned Will about Lord Fanshaw. He had told Will exactly what Edward had said.

Will chuckled. "I can't worry about every person who is mad at me! I would never get any work done," he said, grinning. "Yes, lad, I know Lord Fanshaw isn't happy with me. He knows I don't want him to fence in the land for his sheep. It's no secret."

"But Will," Walter said, "it sounds serious. Please be careful. Maybe you shouldn't talk all the time about how you hate Lord Fanshaw."

"Life is too short to be careful," Will said. Then he looked at Walter. "All right, little friend. If you are that worried, I will try to be more careful. Now run along before *your* father comes after me too."

"Walter?" His father's voice ended Walter's thoughts.

"Yes, sir?" Walter hurried into the next room.

"There you are. I have some cloth for you to deliver to the castle. The Lady Anne needs another new dress. The seamstress needs the cloth today."

"Yes, sir," Walter said slowly. A feeling of dread crept over him. He didn't really want to go back to the castle at all. Not even to see Lady Anne. Thomas might be there. He didn't want to be anywhere near Thomas.

His father looked up at him from his desk. "Aren't you home a bit late for a Thursday?" he asked.

"Uh—I had to stay after and help Master Smyth," Walter fibbed. He couldn't let his father know that he had talked to Will.

"You're not in trouble again, are you?" his father asked. "I hope you're not making up more of those battle stories in your copybook."

"No, sir," Walter said quickly. "Where is the cloth,

Father? I would like to go before it gets dark."

His father handed him the bundle of cloth. Walter hurried out the door. With any luck, he thought, the seamstress would meet him right away. Then he wouldn't have to wait around the castle.

At the castle, the doorkeeper led him to the same little room where he had waited before.

"I'll call the seamstress," he told Walter.

Walter couldn't help thinking of the last time he had waited here. He stared at the grey stone walls. It was silent in the great hall next door. He laid the cloth carefully on the table.

"Oh, it *is* you!" A clear voice broke into his thoughts. Walter looked up to see Lady Anne. She was standing in the doorway, smiling. Smiling? At him?

"Yes, Milady," Walter said. He took off his cap.

"I wanted to ask you a question," she said, coming into the room.

"Yes?" Walter said. What in the world could Lady Anne want?

"Edward told me you have many Latin quotes in your Little Book," she said. "My new tutor wants me to start a Little Book too. Those Latin poets are so dull!" She sighed. "But Edward says you have some good quotes about battles and fighting."

Her cheeks turned a little pink. She took a breath. "May I—may I copy some of your quotes?" she asked, turning a deeper rose.

Walter blinked. Here was Lady Anne—Lord Fanshaw's daughter—asking him for a favor! He could hardly believe it.

"Of—of course," he stammered. "I don't have it with me, though."

"Oh, that's all right," Lady Anne said gratefully. "Just give it to Edward. He can bring it to me."

Not likely, Walter thought. If he gave Edward his Little Book, he'd never see it again. But he couldn't tell Lady Anne how he felt. He thought quickly.

"Actually, I'm using it right now. I have to make up some work in it," Walter lied.

Lady Anne looked at him. She began to smile. "*You* don't think my wonderful brother would do anything to your book, do you?" Her smile grew wider. "That dear, dear boy?" She began to giggle.

Walter laughed in spite of himself.

"That's all right," Lady Anne said. She smiled at Walter. "Just please bring it the next time you deliver some cloth." She paused and then giggled. "I'll make sure I need a new dress very soon!" She turned to go.

"Uh—good-bye, Lady Anne," Walter said.

"Piffle!" she said, turning back. "Call me Anne." She waved and disappeared through the door.

Anne, Walter thought. She said "Anne." He felt light-headed.

Suddenly Walter heard, "For the last time, I *will* not!"

Walter jumped. Loud voices echoed down the hallway.

It was Lord Fanshaw—and Thomas too, he realized. His heart raced. Their heavy footsteps were coming closer. I can't let them see me, he thought. Desperately, he looked around the small room for a place to hide.

The chest—he could hide behind the chest. He raced over to the carved chest. He huddled behind it. His heart was pounding.

Lord Fanshaw and Thomas were in the small room now.

"You greedy, miserly—" Thomas shouted.

"You rotten drunkard!" Lord Fanshaw sneered back.

They walked on into the great hall. Walter wiped his sweaty forehead. Whew! They hadn't seen him.

He peeked around the chest. He couldn't see them in the next room. But he could definitely hear them. They were getting even angrier.

"Even if you *had* been the oldest," Lord Fanshaw was saying, "Father wouldn't have left *anything* to you. You were always a weakling. You never could handle anything. Anything!"

"I'm giving you one last chance," Thomas warned.

Walter's heart thudded. Did Lord Fanshaw have his knights ready? Why didn't he have someone protecting him?

Lord Fanshaw laughed. "What's this?" he mocked. "Are you threatening me again? With your own personal dagger? It has your coat of arms on it, remember? You wouldn't dirty your precious dagger with my blood, would you?" Then Lord Fanshaw laughed again.

Walter froze. There was no mistaking the next sound he heard.

"Unnnh!" Lord Fanshaw grunted.

Walter heard a thud on the stone castle floor. He couldn't breathe.

"Ohhhh! Ohhhhh!" Someone was moaning and gasping for air. Lord Fanshaw! Walter thought in horror. He could imagine Lord Fanshaw, writhing on the floor, blood gushing from his wounds.

Then Walter heard someone else's voice. Someone— one of the servants, maybe—was coming down the other hall. "Lord Fanshaw?" the voice called.

Thomas was trapped. Whoever was coming would definitely see the blood-covered knife Thomas held. Wouldn't he? Walter hoped against hope.

Next, Walter heard a hollow, clanking sound. Then footsteps rushed into the room where Walter was hiding. It must be Thomas! The footsteps stopped.

Walter held his breath. He flattened himself against the chest. If Thomas found him now, he would be dead— just like Lord Fanshaw. Walter's blood ran cold. He was sure Thomas could hear his heart beating. He thought it was going to burst right out of his chest. Please, oh please, Walter begged silently. Go—run—I won't tell anyone! I promise!

"Lord Fanshaw?" the voice repeated, closer now.

Thomas muttered something under his breath. What

was he saying? Then Walter heard Thomas run through the doorway.

"Oh, help! Someone, please help!" screeched the voice from the great hall. "Lord Fanshaw! Lord Fanshaw's been murdered! Help, ho!"

That was it. Walter wasn't staying here one more minute. He ran from the room leaving the cloth where it lay.

He peered around the next corner. No one was in sight. He could make his escape. Walter raced down the halls and out the small door he had used to come into the castle.

He ran across the field, panting. He would have to keep close to the trees. He didn't want anyone from the castle to see him. As he ran, he kept looking behind him. No one was following him—yet.

Walter ran into a little grove of trees. He had to rest. He must have covered a mile at a dead run already. He just needed to rest for a minute. He leaned against a tree to catch his breath.

In his mind, he relived what had just happened. Was it all a bad dream? Oh, if only it were!

He remembered his reason for being at the castle. What would he tell his father about the money for the cloth? He hadn't been paid. Maybe the seamstress would send it to his father. He hoped the seamstress would find the cloth on the table.

Oh no! The cloth was on the table the whole time, he

realized in horror. Thomas had stopped in the room. And he had muttered something. Walter's heart raced beneath his shirt. Thomas must have seen the cloth on the table. Thomas would know Walter had been there.

And Lady Anne knew he had been there too. She had talked to him. What if *he* was charged with the murder of Lord Fanshaw? No one would believe him if he said Thomas was the murderer.

6

The Story Is Out

"Hey!" A voice rang through the grove of trees.

Walter stood stock still. Someone was calling out! Thomas had sent men after him! Now he was going to be caught! He was too young to die!

He looked around desperately. There was nowhere to hide. Maybe if he didn't move a muscle, no one would see him next to the tree.

The bushes thrashed wildly. Someone was crashing through them. A man in a green vest and cap appeared. Walter squeezed his eyes shut waiting for the sword stroke.

"Hey, have you seen a white cow?" the man asked.

Walter almost collapsed in relief.

"Ah, no, I haven't," he said.

The man looked at Walter with curiosity. "Been running, eh? From someone—or to somewhere?"

He sounds suspicious, Walter realized in horror. Once the man heard about the murder, would he remember seeing Walter? He might think *I* am the murderer, Walter worried.

"Um, I'm just in a hurry to get home. My father will punish me if I'm late," Walter said quickly.

The man looked satisfied. "Well, get on with ye, then. Best to get on home where it's safe."

Gratefully, Walter took off at a run. Across more fields, over a stream, always looking behind him, he ran. Finally he got to the lane that ran past his house. He was pretty sure no one had followed him.

But why did he have that strange feeling that he was being watched? Were eyes watching him from high atop the castle walls? Had Thomas seen where he went?

Walter reached his house. He was drenched with sweat. His heart was racing.

Stop it, Walter commanded himself. Calm down. He leaned against the side of his house to gather his thoughts.

Walter knew he had to tell his father about the murder. But first, he had to think about what he'd say.

He could still hear his father's angry voice. "Stay out of the castle's business!" But this wasn't something he could stay out of, even if he tried. His father wouldn't get angry with him, would he? Murder was murder, even at the castle. This was definitely a lot different from all those battles and killings Walter made up in his head. This was real. His hands still shook. He just couldn't believe he had overheard a real murder.

Walter knew he had to organize what he would tell his father. He relived what had happened, step by step. The sounds came back to him clearly. Lord Fanshaw's grunt, the thud, his moans, the sound of the servant approaching, the clank...

Walter's thoughts stopped. He frowned. That sound in the great hall? What would have made that funny clanking sound he had heard?

The dagger—it must have been Thomas' dagger. Of course. His special dagger. It had Thomas' coat of arms on it—his own special signs. Lord Fanshaw had said this. That was why Lord Fanshaw hadn't thought Thomas would really stab him with it. It was too special. What had Thomas done with the dagger to make that sound? Walter puzzled.

Walter went over the events again carefully in his mind. First the stabbing. Then the voice coming down the hall. That must have surprised Thomas. Then the clanking sound. That's it! Walter thought. I have it!

Thomas' dagger would have been covered with blood. The approach of the servant had surprised him. Thomas didn't have time to clean off the blood. That's why he hadn't taken his dagger with him. He couldn't be seen with a bloody dagger. He would have been caught.

So Thomas had to get rid of the dagger in a hurry. But what made that funny sound? What had he done with the dagger?

Walter continued going over the events. Maybe there were more clues.

After the clanking sound, Thomas had run into the room where Walter was hiding. Walter shuddered, remembering. When that voice from the hall called out again, Thomas had run out. But first he had said something. What had he said?

Walter squatted beside the wall. He hugged his knees tightly. He wished he hadn't left the cloth sitting on the table in plain sight. Thomas must have seen it. And Thomas knew Walter was the one who had delivered cloth to the castle the last time.

Thomas would guess that Walter had been around and heard the whole murder. Thomas would find him and kill him. He wouldn't want any witnesses. That was probably what Thomas said. Walter moaned. He was doomed.

There was something else too. Lady Anne knew Walter had been there. They had even talked. She would tell Thomas if he asked. She wouldn't know why Thomas wanted to know.

And Master Edward—he hated Walter. Walter's heart thudded. Edward would say anything to get Walter into trouble.

Then a frightening thought hit Walter. Thomas

wouldn't try to charge him with the murder, would he? Someone who would kill his own brother could definitely think of that.

He took a deep breath and stood up. This was the worst day of his life. It had started out like such a good one too. First, he had pushed Edward into the mud. Then Lady Anne wanted to copy his quotes. But now he was a witness to a murder. And his life was in danger.

All right, he told himself. It's time to tell Father. He opened the door.

"Father?" he called out. His voice was shaking. "Father, are you here?"

"Walter, dear, is that you?" his mother's voice called from the kitchen. Walter walked into the kitchen. His mother was standing at the hearth. A large pot hung over the open flames. She was stirring something in it.

His mother turned and looked at him. Her forehead creased.

"You look white, lad," she said, worried. "Are you well?" She put the spoon down and walked over to Walter.

"You feel warm," she said, feeling Walter's forehead. "You might have a fever." She gently pushed his hair back from his forehead.

"No, Mother," Walter said forcefully. "I'm not sick. I—I—something horrible happened! I—have to tell Father!"

"Tell me what?" his father said, walking into the

room. His father frowned at him. "What did you do—run all the way from the castle?" His father's eyes searched him. "And where's the money?" His father shook his head. "I suppose you're going to tell me you dropped the bag of money? If you did, you're going right back to find it." Robert Poresby folded his arms across his chest.

"Father—Mother—" Walter began. He felt dizzy. He dropped onto a chair. He looked at his parents. His mother looked concerned. His father just looked angry.

"I—I was delivering the cloth to the castle." He stopped and took a deep breath. "I was waiting in a little room for the seamstress. Then I heard voices."

"This sounds like the same story you wanted to tell last time," barked his father. "Can't you make up anything new?"

"No, Father, I mean—this isn't made up," Walter pleaded.

"Robert, let the boy go on," his mother said softly. Walter looked at his mother gratefully.

"Anyway—it was Lord Fanshaw and his brother Thomas. They were arguing again. But this time—this time," Walter stopped. He could hardly say the words aloud. "Thomas stabbed Lord Fanshaw to death!" There! He had said it.

"What?" his parents said at the same time.

"Lord Fanshaw is dead, you say?" his father asked, shocked.

"He was murdered?" his mother asked. Her eyes

were wide. "I can't believe it!"

"I can believe it of that scoundrel brother of his," growled his father.

"What did you do? Did you see it happen?" his mother asked, worried.

"No, I just heard it. They didn't see me. I was in the other room. But," Walter swallowed, "the worst part is, I think Thomas knows I was there, even though he didn't see me."

Robert's face darkened. "He *what?!*"

"Yes," Walter moaned. "I was hiding when he came through the room. But I'm sure he saw the cloth lying on the table. I forgot it was there. And he knows I bring cloth to the castle."

Walter took a breath. "You see, the last time I was at the castle I overheard Thomas threaten Lord Fanshaw. When Thomas stormed out of the great hall, he saw me. He accused me of eavesdropping. It was clear he didn't like witnesses." Walter's voice shook. "That was the story I wanted to tell you before."

Walter continued. "This time, Lady Anne knows I was there too. She talked to me. Thomas will find out. Now I'm a witness to a murder. And the murderer knows it!"

"Oh, my poor darling," his mother cried. She rushed to Walter. She put her arms around him.

"Mother, please," Walter said.

"Now, Mary, no sense in babying the boy," Robert

said. Mary stood back. She patted Walter's head.

"I don't know what to do, Father. Should we tell Constable Hawkins? Will Thomas come after me to kill me?" Walter asked, worried. "Should I stay at home until we know it's safe?"

Robert folded his arms. He paced up and down the room for a few moments. Then he stopped.

"We can't do anything right now," he said. "We don't really know that Thomas knows you were there, right? I think maybe you have let your imagination run away with you again! You and your stories." His father shook his head.

Walter looked away from his father. He stared at the floor. He should have known his father wouldn't believe him. His father never understood. But in his heart, Walter knew Thomas would put two and two together when he saw the cloth.

"There's no sense in worrying about something that hasn't happened yet," Robert said.

"But, Robert—" Mary interrupted.

"Oh, Mary, of course we'll be careful. We'll keep our eyes open for that scoundrel Thomas."

Robert cleared his throat. "But now to the knot of the problem. First of all, no one will believe you about the murder." Robert frowned. "And not just because you are a young boy."

"Father, I'm not *that* young!" Walter protested.

"Hush, dear," his mother said.

His father's mouth tightened. "You are known around the village for all the stories you make up, Walter. Everyone knows what a fanciful imagination you have. You're always telling about duels and battles. People might think you are just making up another story."

"Father!" exclaimed Walter. "That can't be true! People will have to believe me!"

"That's not the strongest reason," Robert went on. He sighed. "I'm afraid a poor clothier's son cannot accuse a lord's brother of murder. You might find yourself in a lot of trouble. You might even be hung for it. It's too bad you have no proof."

Walter sighed, "You're right, Father." He alone had heard the murder and had heard Thomas run out.

"There is something else dangerous about this too," Robert said. He knit his eyebrows together. "As Lord Fanshaw's brother, Thomas will have to blame the murder on someone. He'll pick someone in the village."

Someone in the village. That was it. Thomas could try to blame *him* for the murder. After all, he had been there!

"I think Will Barnes is going to be in a lot of trouble," Robert said slowly.

"Will?" The words shot out of Walter's mouth before he could stop them. "You think *Will* might be accused of the murder?"

Robert Poresby looked carefully at Walter. "Will has been making threats against Lord Fanshaw for weeks.

Everyone knows he is angry about the fencing of the pasture." Robert shook his head. "There's a lesson here, my boy. It's best to keep your opinions to yourself."

No! Walter wanted to shout. His friend Will wasn't a hothead! He was a good person and a good friend. He must find Will quickly. He had to warn him. Will needed to leave Halstead as soon as possible!

But what about *him*? Would Thomas come looking for the only witness to the murder? Would Walter's body be found "accidentally" drowned in the village stream? Would his neck be broken in an "accidental" fall from his horse?

Walter imagined his broken body lying crumpled on the ground. He shuddered.

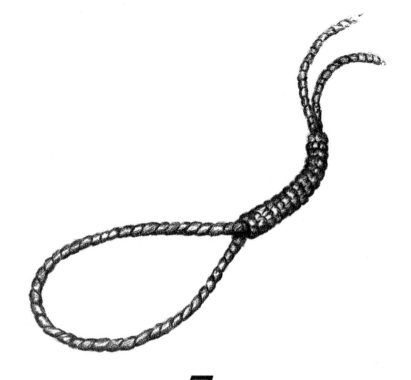

7

Too Late for Will

Later that night, Walter tossed and turned in his bed.

What was that? Was that rustling outside his window? Was it Thomas coming to kill him? A chill ran down his spine. He crept out of bed. He peered out his window into the night.

Gray fog swirled outside—nothing else. Did he hear someone whisper, "Murder...murder...murder..."? He shuddered.

Should he climb out his window? Should he run to warn Will tonight? But wait. What if Thomas or his men were waiting outside? What if they were watching for him? He shuddered. He would wait until tomorrow. He would have to. If he were killed tonight, it wouldn't help anyone, especially Will.

Walter placed his thick walking stick on the floor next to his bed. At least he wouldn't be killed without a fight. Then he got back into bed and pulled the blanket over his head. Maybe he could get some sleep if he pretended no one could see him. He thought about how horrible it would be to be murdered in his own bed.

How he wished the night would end! If only it were already tomorrow afternoon. Then he could find Will and warn him that he might be arrested for Lord Fanshaw's murder. Will had to leave Halstead—and quickly.

Finally, the roosters began crowing. The black sky brightened in the east. Walter rubbed his eyes. His eyelids felt like sandpaper. How he wanted to lie back down in his bed! But today he had to warn Will. He would have to wait until after school. He frowned. School really got in the way of more important things—like saving his friend Will.

Walter knew he would have to be very careful along the lanes on the way to school. Would eyes be watching him from behind hedgerows? Would a horseman in black armor run him down in the road? Walter winced. It wouldn't be hard for Thomas to kill him on the way to school. Walter knew he was in danger, even if his father didn't think so.

Then, if he actually got to school safely, would Edward be there? He shut his eyes. It would be hard to face Edward. He had heard Edward's father's last words. He knew who had murdered him. And it was Edward's own uncle!

Walter shook his head, trying to forget the sound of Lord Fanshaw's dying moans. But he knew he would never forget them. Not for as long as he lived!

An hour later, Walter opened the door to the school-room. Groups of boys stood in the room talking. Their voices were hushed, not noisy as usual. At the front of the room, Master Smyth was wringing his hands. Walter looked carefully around the room. Edward wasn't there. Walter was relieved. He didn't know how he could look Edward in the eye, knowing what he knew.

"Boys, boys," Master Smyth said. Chairs scraped across the wooden floor. The boys settled into their seats. It was quiet in the room. Even the bigger boys his own age had scared looks on their faces.

"I don't think I have to tell you that Lord Fanshaw was murdered yesterday," Master Smyth said. Some of the boys shifted in their seats. A few looked at each other. "Of course, we are all very upset and want to find the murderer. Fortunately, the lord's family has a suspect." Master Smyth stopped.

Walter held his breath. A suspect—already? Could it

possibly be...? Maybe the person who came down the hall had seen Thomas commit the murder! Maybe Walter's nightmare would be over! Please, please, he thought. Walter crossed his fingers for good luck. He squeezed his eyes shut.

"This morning, Constable Hawkins arrested Will Barnes for the murder of Lord Fanshaw," Master Smyth announced. He smiled.

No! Walter almost screamed. Not his friend! Will was not a murderer! He *knew* it!

"It's a relief for everyone to know the murderer has been found. We all know that Will Barnes means trouble. It's high time he was behind bars. And now he'll be hung."

Walter felt his blood run cold. Hung?! He had an image of Will's body hanging from the gallows. No!

"Master Smyth?" Walter put up his hand slowly. Boys weren't supposed to ask questions, he knew. But he *had* to ask this one.

Master Smyth frowned at him. "Poresby?" he barked. "What is it now?"

"Uh—Master Smyth, sir," Walter began. "You say Will—I mean Barnes—will be hung? Won't he have a trial first? What if he isn't guilty?"

Master Smyth laughed. "Poresby," he sneered. "There's not a man in Halstead who hasn't heard Barnes threaten to kill Lord Fanshaw." He looked at Walter over his spectacles. "Trial?" he repeated. "Yes, there will be a trial." Then Master Smyth smiled. It was a slow, wicked smile. "But Barnes will confess first, of course. Then there won't be any need for a trial, will there?"

"Why would he confess when he didn't do it?" Walter burst out.

Master Smyth raised his eyebrows. "Poresby—what is this?" he asked. "Do you think you know more than Constable Hawkins?" He smiled again. "There are ways to make guilty people confess," he said. "Even if they don't want to."

Torture! Walter thought in horror. His friend Will would be tortured. He didn't want to think about the horrible things he had heard about torture. He liked battles, and fighting, and duels—but torture was something different. No one ever held up under the kind of torture he had heard about. Could Will?

"In any event," Master Smyth continued. "There has been a tragedy at the castle. So there will be no school today. School is dismissed."

The boys jumped up. Walter sat in a daze. He had hardly heard Master Smyth's final words.

"Poresby? Dreaming up stories again?" Master Smyth's voice rang in his ear. "If you'd spend the time on your lessons that you spend making up your stories, you'd have a chance of being a student. As it is, you'll be lucky to end up a farmer." Master Smyth snapped his roll book shut. Then he cleaned off his desk.

Walter watched, stunned. It was too late for him to

warn Will. He had betrayed his friend. He had let him down. He could kick himself. Instead of lying sleepless in his bed, he should have sneaked out. He could have run through the moonlight to Will's cottage. He could have awakened Will and told him to leave. After all, his own father had told him Will was in danger. Walter tightened his mouth.

Now Will had been arrested for a murder he didn't commit. Next, he would be tortured until he confessed.

And all the while, Thomas was probably waiting and watching Walter. Even if Will was hung, that didn't mean Thomas would forget about Walter.

So what could Walter do? How could he save his friend as well as himself?

Walter was the last person out of the schoolroom. A small group of boys was gathered just outside.

"Will Barnes, eh?" one of the boys said.

"Aye," said another. "He's always been a troublemaker in the village. My father says so."

"He is not!" Walter blurted.

One of the boys laughed. "Of course *you* would say that," he sneered. "Everyone knows you're his friend. Friends will say anything."

"That's not true!" Walter said angrily. "I know he didn't do it!"

"Really now?" A third boy joined in. "Prove it!"

Walter frowned. He kicked a stone with his shoe.

"See?" one of the boys jeered. "You can't prove it!"

Walter walked away. That was the problem. He couldn't prove it. He had heard the whole terrible thing, but no one would believe him. He knew it. As his father had said, he was just a village boy. Worse, everyone knew he was always making up stories of blood and gore.

How could he accuse Thomas of the murder and prove it?

8

Find the Dagger!

Walter kicked a rock as he headed home from school. "Friends will say anything," the boy had said. I have not even accused Thomas, and already people do not believe me, he thought unhappily.

Walter continued down the muddy road. He saw the jail down a rutted side lane. If only he could talk to Will. Will would know how to get proof. Will always had a plan for everything. But there was no way. This time

Walter had to think for himself.

Poor Will, locked up in Constable Hawkins' tiny jail. Were they already torturing him? Walter shuddered. He didn't have much time.

Proof, his father had said. He needed proof. How could he prove that Thomas had killed his brother? Walter walked slowly down the road looking at the little shops.

There it was! Walter stopped. That was the answer! Right in front of him. Harry the butcher was grinding his knives through the open door of his shop. Knives—the dagger! Walter had to find where Thomas had hidden the bloody dagger!

If he found the dagger, people would believe his story! After all, the dagger had Thomas' emblem on it— his own personal coat of arms. That would mark it as his.

And there should still be bloodstains on it. Walter shuddered. Thomas had been surprised by the voice right after he stabbed his brother. He certainly hadn't had time to clean off the bloodstains. Walter felt sick.

His heart raced. All he had to do was find the dagger. He needed witnesses there too. He had to find the dagger with people watching. Better yet, Constable Hawkins should see him find the dagger. Then the constable could see for himself!

The constable would arrest Thomas for the murder. Will would go free. Walter would be safe. Walter didn't realize he was grinning.

"How are ye, lad?" Harry the butcher called to him, grinning back. "Like to take a turn with these knives?" he joked.

"No, thank you kindly," Walter said quickly. He waved to Harry and hurried on. He couldn't imagine sharpening knives right now. Every whine of the whetstone reminded him of the murder. Lord Fanshaw's groans still haunted him. All that blood in the butcher shop too. No, he didn't need to be around any more blood.

The dagger—he had to find the dagger. Where could Thomas have hidden it? Walter sat down on a tree stump. He had to think hard.

Walter crinkled his forehead. He thought carefully about that horrible afternoon.

Now he had it! Of course! The funny clanking sound from the great hall. Suddenly, Walter knew what he had to do. Somehow, he had to get back to the castle and into the great hall. There must be something there that a dagger could be hidden in—something that would make a clanking noise.

But what if the dagger were no longer there? What if Thomas had gone back for his dagger? Walter could be too late. The dagger might already be gone. Walter had been too late to warn Will. Please don't let me be too late again, he worried.

Walter needed a plan. How was he going to get to the castle? What excuse did he have? Lady Anne wanted to copy his Little Book, true. But she wouldn't want to see him today. She would be in mourning over her murdered father. Walter felt a little sadness sweep through him. It was too bad her father was dead. Lady Anne seemed nice. Sure, she was spoiled. But she wasn't as bad as that nasty brother of hers.

Then he had it. The cloth! he thought. He hadn't been paid for the cloth. He had dropped it on the table. Then he had run after the murder. No, on second thought... Walter frowned. He couldn't go asking anyone at the castle for money today. Everyone in the castle would be weeping and wailing. It would be rude to ask for money at this sad time.

Walter stood up. Maybe by the time he got home he would think of a plan. He slung his bookstrap over his shoulder and headed down the road.

Did he just see a shadow dart between two shops? Was someone following him? Walter's pulse raced. He had almost forgotten! Will had been arrested. But that didn't mean Thomas would stop looking for Walter.

Wasn't Walter the only real witness? Wasn't Walter the only person who could say, "Thomas killed Lord Fanshaw!"? Wasn't Walter the only one who knew the truth? Walter could send Thomas to the chopping block if he could get people to believe him.

Walter hurried. There was another problem—a big one. There was no doubt in his mind that Thomas didn't want a living witness. Walter had to go back to the castle to find the dagger. But *if* he went back, would Thomas be there, waiting for him?

"Glad you're back, my boy," Thomas would say. His hand would twitch at his dagger.

Would Thomas strangle Walter in some dark hallway? Would he push Walter down steep tower stairs? Would he lock Walter up in the dank, mossy dungeon where he would never again see the light of day?

Walter swallowed hard. He had to find a way to get to the castle. But he had to pray that Thomas wouldn't be there. Maybe Thomas had fled the country like Will said he would. If only he had!

Walter looked from side to side. He walked quickly down the middle of the lane. That way, no one would be able to jump out and surprise him. His pulse kept time with his steps. Thump-THUMP, thump-THUMP!

Thankfully, Walter finally turned into the lane leading past his house. His steps quickened. There was his door! He was home. Walter sighed in relief. He put his hand on the latch.

But he hadn't thought of a plan yet. He had to find the dagger before something happened to Will. Or to him.

9

The Giant Vase

"Mother!" Walter called. He slammed the door.

"Yes, Walter?" His mother came around the corner. "Walter! What are you doing home from school?" she asked in surprise. "Is everything all right?"

Walter dropped his Little Book on the table. "Master Smyth dismissed school because of Lord Fanshaw's death yesterday."

"Ah, yes," his mother said. She looked sad. "Those

two poor babies. Their mother just died last year. And now their father."

Two babies? Walter wondered. Then he realized that his mother was talking about Lady Anne and Master Edward. Hmph! he almost snorted. Master Edward was a baby, all right. But not the kind his mother meant.

"We should go to the castle," his mother said. "The villagers will be going today. We can take something to the family. We should pay our respects to Lady Anne and Master Edward."

Walter couldn't believe his luck. His mother wanted to go to the castle! He had an excuse to go! He could look for the dagger!

"The funeral is today?" Walter asked.

"No. This is too early for a funeral. There are many arrangements to be made first. They have to get the body ready," his mother said. "Lord Fanshaw was important. Many lords and ladies will want to come. They need time to travel here."

"What will we take to Lady Anne and Master Edward?" Walter asked.

"Some nice cloth, your father said. He will meet us there," Walter's mother answered.

"Let's go, then," Walter said. He headed toward the door. There was no time to lose. He had to prove who the real murderer was and save Will from torture and a confession.

"You're very eager to go," his mother said. "Why?"

"Oh." Walter looked down at the floor. What excuse

would his mother believe? To his surprise, he felt his face turning warm. Was he blushing? "Ah—Lady Anne—I—uh—I've talked to her. She's been nice," he stammered.

His mother smiled. "That's very kind of you, Walter." She bundled up some fine wool. "Then let us go."

Walter's mother chattered as they walked. Walter wasn't listening. He was thinking about how he would act in the great hall. He couldn't act like he was looking for something. He mustn't draw attention to himself.

And what if Thomas were there? Would Walter be in danger? Surely not with so many people around.

They arrived at the castle. Several other villagers were leaving. Walter's mother exchanged greetings with them. Walter and his mother passed by the huge portcullis and main door. They found the servants' door and knocked.

"Yes?" the doorkeeper asked.

"We are here to pay our respects," Walter announced.

"To the Lady Anne and Master Edward," added his mother.

"They are in the great hall," the doorkeeper said. He led them through the corridors.

There was a line of villagers waiting. The line of people started in the great hall. Villagers spilled into the little room where Walter had hidden at the time of the murder. People talked in whispers.

Walter's stomach tied into a knot. Here he was—right where the murder had happened. He edged over to the arched doorway leading into the great hall. Casually, he leaned against the arch. That way he could see into the next room.

Thankfully, Thomas was nowhere in sight. Lady Anne and Master Edward were there. They stood in front of the huge hearth. Lady Anne's eyes were red. Master Edward's face was stony. Ladies curtsied to them. Men bowed. A few villagers exchanged some words with them. Flowers and gifts loaded a gilded table next to them.

Now what would Thomas have done with that dagger? Walter wondered. He looked carefully at everything. Tapestries hung on the walls. Some chairs were arranged next to chests. The huge table stood next to Lady Anne and Master Edward. A fire blazed in the hearth behind them. The firelight flickered and shone on the huge vase next to it.

The vase! That was it! It could have made the clanking sound if Thomas had dropped his dagger into it!

Walter's heart pounded. Was the dagger still there? he wondered. He had to find out.

Luckily, the line of villagers passed right next to the vase! Walter could look down into it as he passed by. Then maybe he would see the dagger!

The line moved slowly. Too slowly, Walter thought. Finally, he and his mother reached Lady Anne.

His mother began talking with Lady Anne. Walter took a couple of steps across the straw-covered floor toward the vase. It was enormous. It looked very heavy.

"What are you doing?" asked Lady Anne. She had finished talking to his mother.

Walter felt color come to his cheeks. "I—ah—I was interested in this vase," he said.

Lady Anne looked puzzled. "Really?" She walked toward it. "Why?"

Walter quickly followed her. "It—ah—I thought I saw battle scenes painted on it," he fibbed. "I just wanted a closer look."

"Oh," Anne said. "Of course. You're always telling those stories about battles and fighting. My brother said that's what your quotes are about too." She gave him a sad smile.

Walter stood next to the vase. It was half his height. He looked down inside it. Did he see something gleaming inside? Was there a glint of metal at the bottom? Was that—could it be the dagger? Yes—he was almost sure of it! He wanted to yell and shout and jump up and down. But he couldn't. He clenched his fists in excitement.

"What do you see in there?" Anne asked, curiously. "I thought you were interested in the *outside* of the vase."

"Oh, nothing," Walter said. He stood back from the vase. He pretended to study the outside. "It's not what I thought," he said, trying to sound disappointed.

"Is everything all right?" Anne asked him. She looked at him strangely.

"Yes," Walter said joyfully. Then he could have bitten

his tongue. Here Lady Anne's father had just been murdered. And he was acting happy. Quickly, he rearranged his face. He tried to look sad.

"Uh—I'm—I'm sorry about your father, Lady Anne," he choked out.

Lady Anne bit her lip. Her eyes filled with tears. She looked down at her velvet shoes.

"Thank you," she said.

Walter tried to think of something cheerful.

"I—I'll bring you my Little Book soon," he stuttered.

Anne took a breath. "That would be nice," she said, forcing a smile. "Would you tell me how you find your quotes? My tutor wants me to have a lot," she sighed. "Although right now, that is the last thing I want to be doing."

Walter looked down at the stone floor. After all, her father had been murdered yesterday. He felt sorry for her, even if Lord Fanshaw had not been the best of men.

Next was Master Edward—his favorite. His mother was still talking to him. Good. Lady Anne was receiving another villager. Walter had a moment to plan what to do next.

Why hadn't Thomas gotten the knife out? Where was Thomas now? Was he gone? Had he left the country? Walter looked over at the vase again. The opening of the vase was pretty small.

Maybe that was it! Thomas' hand might have been too big. He may not have been able to reach inside the opening to get the dagger back out.

Walter was still puzzled. Why hadn't Thomas tried to shake the knife out of the vase? Walter wondered. Well, the vase was huge. So it must be very heavy. It would be difficult for one man to tip it on its side. No one could do that in a hurry. Also, the opening at the top of the vase was very narrow. It would be hard for the knife to drop out, even if the vase were held upside down. And that wouldn't be easy for one man to do.

Suppose Thomas returned to the castle for the weapon after the murder. He would need a time when no one would surprise him while he worked to get the weapon out. That would be nearly impossible. Lots of people walked through the great hall all the time.

Walter's heart leaped. Thomas' fist would have been too big to get through the opening. But *his* hand should be able to pull the dagger out!

Suddenly Master Edward's voice broke into his thoughts.

"Poresby! Are you deaf as well as dumb?" Edward said rudely.

"What?" Walter asked.

"I've been trying to get your attention," Edward almost shouted. "Are you making up more of those stupid stories again?"

It was hard to be nice to Edward—even if his father had just been murdered. Walter balled up his fists. He would just ignore what Edward said.

"I'm sorry about your father," Walter said.

"Peasants are sorry too?" Edward said, mockingly.

Peasant! Walter thought angrily. There was that word again. He wouldn't punch Edward's fat face today though. But only because his father had just died. Walter set his jaw.

"I'm no peasant," Walter said through clenched teeth.

Edward sneered. "I'm not sure I like the idea of you coming to the castle. After all, you are the murderer's friend. And his confession will be quick, I hear." Edward paused. His eyes looked cruelly at Walter. "I hope Will takes a long time to hang."

Walter's face grew hot. "Will is not a murderer! He didn't do it!" he said angrily. "I'm sorry your father's dead—but Will didn't do it!"

Edward's face crumpled a bit. He really must have cared about his father, Walter thought in surprise. It was hard to believe Edward could care about anyone but himself.

Edward took a deep breath. "I don't know why you act so sure," he said. "Unless it's because he's your friend. Oh, who cares? You'd make up anything. Everyone knows *that!*"

That does it, Walter told himself. That comment doesn't deserve an answer. He turned and left Edward standing there. He walked over to his mother's side.

"Walter, your father is here," his mother said. "He's in line, now. We'll wait for him." They stepped aside.

Walter's eyes returned to the vase. He had to decide what he was going to do about the dagger. He wanted to walk over, reach in, and pull out the dagger. But he needed witnesses—especially Constable Hawkins. Walter scanned the crowd. No Constable Hawkins. His heart beat rapidly.

A scary thought entered Walter's mind. Thomas could walk in any minute. Then what would happen? Walter wondered in dread. His palms felt sweaty. He had taken a big chance by coming here today.

"It's hard to believe Lord Fanshaw is gone," his mother was saying. "He was alive just yesterday, when you were here."

"Yesterday?" asked a slow voice from the arched doorway. "*You* were here *yesterday?*"

Walter turned to face the voice. His worst nightmare. It was Thomas.

10

A True Story

"You were here *yesterday?"* Thomas repeated. His eyes narrowed.

Walter's heart stopped. He sensed his mother stiffen beside him. His father was at the other end of the room. But even his father couldn't protect him against Thomas. What was he going to do? Was he in danger? Should he run?

"Yes," Walter said loudly. He forced a smile. "I came and left some cloth for the seamstress. I often do that," he said.

"You just left it? You didn't wait for your money?" Thomas asked. He stared at Walter from under heavy eyebrows.

"No. My father was angry with me. I was late. I had to hurry home," Walter said, breathlessly.

"That's right," his mother said. Her voice shook. "The boy's right."

Thomas looked as if he didn't believe a word they were saying.

"In fact, I need to talk to my father right now," Walter said. He pointed to Robert Poresby across the room. Then he made a face. "He is always angry with me. I forgot to do my chores again." He sighed.

Thomas frowned. He looked coldly at Walter. "You'd better get over there then. And don't come back to the castle. You don't belong here," he said evilly. "And you know it."

"Yes, Milord," Walter said quickly. He took his mother by the hand. Just before they rushed around the corner out of the great hall, Walter glanced back.

Thomas was still glaring at him, his arms folded.

Walter's heart pumped furiously. Thomas didn't believe him. He knew it! Thomas would be waiting somewhere, sometime, to kill him. Walter would be dead soon if he couldn't prove Thomas was the murderer—and quickly.

Umph! Walter bumped into a large person.

"Ease up! Ease up, lad!" Constable Hawkins' voice was the most welcome sound Walter had ever heard.

"What's your hurry, Walter? Has someone stolen some cloth from your father? Or have sheep been stolen?"

"Constable Hawkins—no!" Walter gasped. "It's worse than that! I know who murdered Lord Fanshaw—and I can prove it—I think!"

Constable Hawkins shook his head and smiled. "Now, lad, is this another one of your stories? This is no laughing matter, you know. We've got Will Barnes locked up. It doesn't look good for him, either." He sighed. "You can't hope to save your friend with some wild story."

"No!" Walter shouted. "It's not a story! If you'll just come with me for a minute, I can show you! I can prove who the murderer is! Follow me—into the great hall—now!" Walter let go of his mother's hand. He grabbed the constable's arm.

"Push ahead of everyone?" Constable Hawkins asked. He frowned. "We can't do that."

"We *have* to! " Walter took a deep breath. "I overheard Thomas murder Lord Fanshaw!"

"*What?!*" Constable Hawkins exclaimed. "His own brother? You overheard it? And you can prove it?"

"I was delivering cloth. I heard them fighting. I'd heard them fight before. Lord Fanshaw wouldn't give Thomas more money. So Thomas threatened to kill him. Thomas stabbed him with his dagger. Then someone was about to come in and find Thomas. So he dropped the dagger into the big vase in the great hall. Then he ran from the room." Walter's words tumbled out.

"So," Constable Hawkins looked carefully at Walter, "how can you prove this?"

"By finding the dagger!" Walter said excitedly. "I can get the dagger out of the vase. It has Thomas' coat of arms on it. And—" he paused "—and it should still have bloodstains on it too!"

"This is all very interesting," said Constable Hawkins. "But why are you in such a rush about it?"

"Because," Walter said, "I want to save Will. And Thomas knows that I know he is the murderer. He will kill me too! I know it!" Walter looked nervously over his shoulder. Thomas was standing next to the giant vase in the great hall. Was he guarding it?

"Well, we can't have that—*if* it's true," Constable Hawkins said. "I suppose it's worth a try. But if this is one of your wild stories..." he frowned at Walter.

"No, sir! I promise it isn't! But, sir, Thomas is standing right next to the vase." Walter scanned the people around him. The villagers were talking quietly among themselves. No one was listening to Walter.

"Are there any men we can take with us—just in case?" Walter begged. "Thomas will be terribly angry!"

Constable Hawkins rounded up some sturdy men. Walter and the others pushed their way through the crowd. Some people grumbled.

"Hey, wait your turn," muttered one man.

"We've been here waiting," complained another.

"Murder investigation," said Constable Hawkins quietly.

The crowd let the Constable and his men through.

Quickly and silently, they moved into the great hall. Their swords swung at their sides.

Walter stared at the vase flickering in the firelight. His heart thudded.

"What is *this*, Constable?" Thomas' voice made Walter jump. "In such a hurry to pay your respects to the family?" he said sarcastically. "And the village pup, again?" he added, staring at Walter. Walter felt as if Thomas' eyes were boring a hole right through his fore-head.

"We are investigating further, sire," Constable Hawkins said smoothly.

"Can't you let the dead rest in peace?" Thomas asked bitterly. Thomas' forehead was beaded with sweat, Walter noticed.

Walter's own palms were wet with fear. Here he was, face-to-face with the enemy. What if Thomas wouldn't let him near the vase?

"That's what we hope to do, sire," Constable said. He motioned to the men. They moved between Thomas and the vase. "Lad?" Constable motioned to Walter. "Let's see this now."

The room was silent. Walter felt light-headed. He swallowed hard. He walked up to the vase. He leaned over and put his hand inside. Nothing! he thought in horror.

No—wait! Yes! *Yes!* His fingers touched cold metal! It was the handle of the dagger! He grabbed it. Carefully, he brought the dagger up to the opening of the vase. He straightened his fingers and wedged them through the opening.

"Unh!" he said. He had it! Triumphantly he held it high! Thomas' coat of arms shone in the firelight. There were dark stains all over the blade.

"Aaaah!" Thomas cried out in rage. He lunged at Walter. Instantly, the men grabbed him. They pinned his arms behind him.

"You miserable cur!" shouted Thomas. "You'll die for this!"

"No, sire," said Constable Hawkins. "I believe *you* will die for this." He turned to Walter. "Good work, lad."

Walter looked proudly at the dagger in his hand. He had done it! He had saved his friend! This wasn't just a story he had made up, either. This was real!